Little Pig

JOINS THE BAND

David Hyde Costello

ini Charlesbridge

For Keating and Sagan—
and littlest ones everywhere

Published by Charlesbridge
85 Main Street
Watertown, MA 02472
(617) 926-0329
www.charlesbridge.com

Library of Congress Cataloging-in-Publication Data
Costello, David Hyde.
    Little Pig joins the band / David Hyde Costello.
        p. cm.
    Summary: When Little Pig tries to join his grandpa, brothers, and sisters in a
marching band he discovers that, although he is too small for any of the available
instruments, he can still play an important role.
    ISBN 978-1-58089-264-3 (reinforced for library use)
[1. Marching bands—Fiction. 2. Bands (Music)—Fiction. 3. Conductors (Music)—Fiction.
4. Size—Fiction. 5. Brothers and sisters—Fiction. 6. Pigs—Fiction.] I. Title.
PZ7.C82283Lit 2011
[E]—dc22   2010007582

Printed in China
(hc) 10 9 8 7 6 5 4 3 2 1

Illustrations done in ink and watercolor on Strathmore cold-press watercolor paper
Display type created by Ryan O'Rourke and text type set in Palatino Sans Informal
Color separations by Chroma Graphics, Singapore
Printed and bound February 2011 by Yangjiang Millenium Litho Ltd.
    in Yangjiang, Guangdong, China
Production supervision by Brian G. Walker
Designed by Susan Mallory Sherman

C'mon, Little Pig!

Sometimes Little Pig didn't like being little,

or even being called Little Pig.

My name is Jacob!

When his brothers and sisters got out
Grandpa's old marching-band instruments,

Little Pig looked for something he could play.

Little Pig was too little to play the drum,

so Margie played the drum.

Little Pig was too little to play the trombone,

so Peter played the trombone.

Little Pig was too little to play the trumpet,

so Sally played the trumpet.

Little Pig was too little to play the . . .

So Tiny played the tuba.

Little Pig was just too little to join the band.

He watched everyone marching around the house.

He listened to the music they were playing.

And then . . .

Little Pig knew what the problem was—the band needed a leader!

Did somebody lose a button?

Little Pig gave the signal, and off they marched!